Goldie's Lox
and the Three Bagels

Goldie's Lox
and the Three Bagels

~ FRACTURED JEWISH FAIRY TALES ~

Jeffrey & *Lila* Dubinsky

ILLUSTRATIONS BY DICK SIEGEL

CITADEL PRESS
Kensington Publishing Corp.
www.kensingtonbooks.com

CITADEL PRESS BOOKS are published by

Kensington Publishing Corp.
850 Third Avenue
New York, NY 10022

All Kensington titles, imprints, and distributed lines are available at
special quantity discounts for bulk purchases for sales promotions,
premiums, fund-raising, educational, or institutional use. Special book
excerpts or customized printings can also be created to fit specific needs.
For details, write or phone the office of the Kensington special sales
manager: Kensington Publishing Corp., 850 Third Avenue, New York,
NY 10022, attn: Special Sales Department;
phone 1-800-221-2647.

CITADEL PRESS and the Citadel logo are Reg. U.S. Pat. & TM Off.

First printing: October 2007

10 9 8 7 6 5 4 3 2 1

Printed in the United States of America

Library of Congress Control Number: 2007929061

ISBN-13: 978-0-8065-2861-8
ISBN-10: 0-8065-2861-3

Contents

Goldie's Lox
and the Three Bagels

Shlepping Beauty

ack in the days when women worked but did not have careers—except for the matchmaker, who possessed the power of clergy with none of the accountability—there dwelt in a remote hamlet a *maidel* named Aziza who worked at the post office and delivered the mail.

Aziza was hired because she was honest as well as pure, not like the previous clerk who was said to have stolen money orders, checks, and even dimes being sent to plant trees in Israel, the *goniff*!

Because she worked so hard and so diligently, carting her heavy letter bag around the village, Aziza soon earned the nickname of *Shlepping* Beauty.

Spying on Aziza as she made her rounds, the local matchmaker was unhappy to see how many young men sent themselves letters just so the *shainkeit* blonde would stop by each day.

"As long as this *kurveh* keeps unloading sacks around town, no man will entertain proposals!" the crone moaned. "I'll go broke!"

Nor was the matchmaker so *fardrai zich dem kop*. One of her best prospects was Phil, a prince of a boy who gave riding lessons—and more to the *alteh moids*, it was said, if the price was right—who seemed particularly smitten by the letter carrier.

Acting quickly, the matchmaker ordered hundreds of flyers advertising her services. Though it pained her to spend the money, she knew it would pain Aziza even more to *shlep* them door-to-door.

So it came to pass that one bright morning at the end of the week, when she was already tired, the young woman set out with her deliveries, which included bundles of pamphlets—not postcards like other local merchants, and printed on heavy fifty-pound coated stock—advertising the services of Ring Finger to Prick Matchmaking Services.

At two in the afternoon, by which time Aziza was usually done, she was only halfway through the route. Her shoulders ached, her legs were trembling, her feet were sore, and her vision was not so hot, for she thought the pole outside the barbershop had grown a head—that of the matchmaker.

But Aziza pressed on, eventually reaching the woods that separated the town from the post office. Unaccustomed to navigating the forest when the sun was setting, she soon lost her way. Crossing a cute pink bridge, she found herself in an unfamiliar thicket of thornbushes.

"Thank God I wore my *gotkes*," she said, for the thick undergarment protected her legs from the prickles.

Before very long, Aziza was so exhausted that she stopped and burst into tears. Suddenly, three *faigelahs* appeared from the darkness. They were holding their clothing and apparently had been on a botanical outing, for one of them said something about having come out here for a daisy chain with a woodsman.

"I'm sorry," sobbed the tired Aziza, "but I'm lost. Can you direct me to the post office?"

"*Bubeleh*, you are so off course!" said one of the men who was bronzed without tan lines. "This is Fairy Island!"

"*Oy*," sighed the girl.

Falling wearily to the ground, her bag fell open beside some unripe seedpods that oozed white sap. Out tumbled a postcard that one of the men eyed with interest.

"Who's the *shtrudel* in chaps?" he asked.

"That's an advertisement for Phil the horseman," Aziza replied.

"Is that his profession or—"

"Of course, his profession," Aziza said. "What else?"

The men tittered but said nothing.

"If only Phil were here, he would escort me safely home," the young woman went on.

"Tell you what," said one of the men. "Why don't we go and get your friend?"

"Oh, would you?" she asked.

"Even if we have to dress like a horse to get his attention!" said one.

"And kidnap him!" said the second.

"And get hung like a horse if need be," said the third.

"But tell me," Aziza said pensively. "If you know the way, why don't you just take me home?"

"Because you look tired," said the man, hiding a grin behind his mouth. "You should rest."

Aziza looked around warily.

"Oh, you're perfectly safe here," said another. "You have nothing that anyone on Fairy Island might want, except for those silk *gotkes* and maybe the post-card—which I'll take for reference."

"Well, I am exhausted," the girl admitted. "Maybe I'll take a little *dremel*."

So saying, the girl laid her head on her letter bag, but within moments she was in a deep sleep, dreaming that she was a princess in a castle with nothing to do but sing, pick flowers, and talk to animals.

Meanwhile, the three *faigelahs* went romping through the woods, singing, picking flowers, and talking to animals. Because it was dark when they reached the village, they went directly to a cute bed and breakfast where they slept in—carelessly forgetting their mission as they went window-shopping the next morning.

Back in the woods, the wickedly exhausted Aziza continued to sleep and sleep, for the pods beside her were poppies and their proximity had sedated her. All the while the bushes grew thicker and her sleep grew deeper and the wind took the contents of her letter bag here and there.

Yet her absence had not gone unnoticed. Phil was particularly distracted, for he had not received any mail for several days. Asking around the village, he learned that no one else had seen Shlepping Beauty either.

"She could be shacking up with Mordecai in the woods," suggested the matchmaker.

"I hear she fancies his timber."

Phil was not so sure, especially after what he overheard three strange men in the street saying about the woodsman and his parties.

Phil decided to ride out to the post office to see what had happened to the beautiful young girl—and his mail, since he was the rare Jew who did not like to wait until the last possible moment to pay his bills.

As he rode through town, one of the *faigelahs* happened to look up from brunch.

"*Kuck!*" he cried as he recognized the chaps.

"Not my scene," said Arumloifer, a young man they had invited to join them.

"The girl!"

"Only my good friends call me that!" sneered the guest.

"No, Shlepping Beauty!" he wailed.

"*Gevalt!*" shouted the other two *faigelahs* in unison.

Flying from the charming outdoor café, the men whistled after the horseman. Accustomed as he was to being whistled at by women, the attention of the men was new and not unintriguing. Phil stayed his horse, that wanted very much to flee, and turned to hear what all the chirping was about.

"She's in trouble!" one of the *faigelahs* shouted.

"Which of you?" Phil asked.

"We just used that joke!" said Arumloifer, rolling his eyes.

"Not us, silly!" cooed the man. "Shlepping Beauty!"

"Where is she?" the equestrian demanded. "What has happened?"

The *faigelahs* spoke at once, with speed and affectations to which his ear was unaccustomed. Pointing to one and telling him to start again, slowly, Phil listened to how the mail carrier had gotten lost and fallen asleep deep in the woods.

Driving heel to rib that set the horse's legs—and the *faigelah*'s hearts—at a gallop, Phil rode into the forest where he soon spotted the matchmaker's flyers. Collecting them as he rode, but oblivious to the irony that the instrument of Aziza's exhaustion and their separation should also lead to their reunification, Phil finally came to the thornbushes where Shlepping Beauty lay.

Hacking through the gnarled hedge with a polo mallet—which he kept in case he was someplace where he needed to pass—Phil reached her side. Dismounting, Phil kissed her. He had done that a little backwards, he knew, but reading from right to left wasn't exactly normal either.

Shlepping Beauty opened her eyes and smiled when she saw Phil.

"Why are my *gotkes* between your legs?" she enquired, still groggy from the opiate.

Phil reddened and tossed them aside. "They, uh . . . were torn by the thorns."

"Oh," she said. "That would also explain the blood."

The horseman nodded as he scooped Aziza from the poppies. She was grateful to be deflowered and her head cleared quickly.

The two rode back to the village, where the three *faigelahs* rejoiced, for they could now go shopping for gowns to wear at the wedding.

Shlepping Beauty and her prince were wed, after which she turned her business over to the three *faigelahs* who, she was assured, would diligently attend to the mails. So they did, giving particular attention to larger packages. As for the matchmaker, she moved to Fairy Island where she went into business arranging something called "hookups." They were shorter term and cheaper, but she made up for that in bulk.

And they all lived happily ever after, you should live so.

Hamish and Gretel

ot far enough from a great forest, that you shouldn't know from, dwelt a poor wood-cutter with his wife and their two children. The boy, months shy of being a man, was called Hamish because he was so friendly, and the younger girl was named Gretel because—if you must know—they had a wealthy aunt in Pskov named Gertie who they hoped this would impress. It didn't; go know.

The woodsman was not such a good provider, as his mother-in-law had predicted, and when drought fell upon the land, he could no longer give his family their daily bread.

"What is to become of us?" moaned his wife as they lay in bed one night. "How are we to feed Hamish and his *farbissoner* sister?"

"You could try eating a little less," her husband suggested, glancing at her overample bosom.

"When I worry, I eat!" she snapped.

"You should have married the butcher," her husband sighed.

"Should! Should! You should have kept your *shmekel* buttoned," she replied, thinking of that fateful night after drinking too much Mogen David at the Schwartz bat mitzvah. "A *broch*," she said. "We must now do like the good book says."

"Stone the children?"

"Where will we find stones?" his wife snarled. "You used them all to build this Winter Palace, this Taj Mahal! No. Tomorrow morning we will take our children out into the wilderness, leave them there with a loaf of bread, and let God provide the rest."

The woodcutter knew better than to argue with his wife when she was in a mood, so they went to bed. He would talk sense to her in the morning, when she was busy trying to get into her girdle and would agree to anything in exchange for his help.

But the two children—who had put cheese on the cow's tongue sandwich they had had for dinner and could not sleep for the wind they broke—had heard everything. Feeling guilty because they were Jewish, not because they had done anything, the two waited until their parents were asleep. Then, tucking a loaf of bread in the pocket of his coat, Hamish took his sister by the hand and led her deep into the woods.

"Are we going back to where you made that calf out of mud, to revel unclean—?" Gretel inquired.

"Uh . . . no," Hamish replied quickly. "But we are going to find a land flowing with milk and honey."

"Shouldn't you stop and get directions?" she nagged.

Hamish ignored her, for, as she continued to speak, there was aught else to do. Guided by the light of the full moon, he picked his way through unfamiliar copses—leaving behind a trail made from crumbs of bread just in case he got all *tsedrait in kop* and ended up in Novgorod where there were Cossacks.

They walked and walked and walked until Hamish ran out of bread and Gretel ran out of patience.

"We're going back!" she said, sounding more like her mother than Hamish had ever heard before and which was scarier than the dark night.

Unfortunately, as she turned to follow the trail of breadcrumbs, she found—much to her horror—that they had been followed by Moishe who cared for horses at the inn and had eaten every morsel.

"It's a poor groom!" Hamish shouted, scaring Moishe who ran off before they could get directions home.

"We're lost and that's all you have to say?" Gretel screamed.

"*Zay gezunt!*" Hamish yelled after him, for he was that kind of boy.

Lost and without food or money, Hamish and Gretel had no choice but to continue their journey. Finally, when the moon was as low as a Hassid's hemline, Hamish saw it.

"Look!" he cried, pointing.

"*Shoyn tsayt*," Gretel said, unimpressed. "Your finger is out of your nose."

"No, there! A cottage!"

Sure enough, the first light of dawn revealed a little house that was unlike any they had ever seen. It was built of *latkes* and covered with macaroons. The two ran over and began pulling at the cookies, which they were actually hungry enough to eat. Noticing that the mortar was applesauce, Hamish promptly switched to the potato shingles.

"*Aleychem shalom!*" came a raspy voice from behind him.

Hamish turned and saw a cat and a cigarette. Between them was a face that belonged on a golem.

"Grandma?" asked Hamish.

But then the smoke cleared, and he saw that it was not Tillie Obolensky but someone who only smelled like her. Hamish reflexively withdrew to protect his cheeks, before realizing that they were entirely safe.

"*Nosh, nosh, nosh.* Who is *noshing* at my house?" she cackled.

Hamish and Gretel stopped eating at once. Behind them, a *halvah* window frame fell from the partly eaten wall. The *matzoh* shutters shattered upon hitting the ground.

"Look!" shouted Hamish. "I found the *afikomen!*"

Gretel was too frightened to sneer at him.

"Actually," Hamish continued, "we are the Brill-steins, one of the lost tribes of—"

"*Sha!*" the crone shouted. "My lawyer will be in touch about the window. Now, no more of your *bobe mayses!* If you're hungry, come inside. People call me *Tanta* Rose. I have chicken soup."

Startled by the woman's generosity, the children followed her inside.

"Maybe we can settle about the window," Hamish whispered hopefully to his sister.

"How?"

"I'll think of something," Hamish said. He looked at the old woman's legs, which protruded from her housedress like tree stumps, the stockings bunched below her knobbed knees. The thought of any act performed in their proximity, even massaging her feet, was so *chalushisdick* that he began reciting his *haftorah* just to chase away the image.

The woman gestured toward a table. It was cov-

ered with a cloth that looked like it hadn't been changed since the year *gimel.* Wax from countless Sabbaths hung from silver candlesticks in the center. Soot from the fireplace coated the furniture.

"You do a lot of cooking," Hamish observed, his eyes settling on a huge, bubbling cauldron in the hearth.

The woman shrugged. "The children never call. Besides *Hadassah* meetings and Mah Jongg, what else is there to do? That's how I came to build this house. There was no one to take home leftovers, and who wants to waste? But sit," she went on. "You must be famished."

As you are *farmisht,* Hamish thought as he took a seat at the table.

His sister joined him as the woman filled bowls— her everyday bowls, not even the ones for company— with chicken soup from the cauldron.

"Don't worry, it's all *kashruit,*" the woman said. "I do it myself, you see. Drain the little boys—did I say boys?" she laughed. "I mean, the little chickens. If you want it done right, you know what they say!"

As the slow-moving *yenta* started to shuffle back, Gretel realized something. Quick like a bunny, the girl jumped from her seat, ran toward their hostess, and, with a *zetz* like you wouldn't believe, knocked the woman into the fire.

"*A shvartz yor!*" the old woman screeched as she exploded in flames, her dry flesh going up like the price of a suit bought retail.

"Why did you do that?" Hamish cried. "We hadn't eaten!"

"This was no Tanta Rose," Gretel assured him. "She was a witch."

"How do you know?"

"Look around you," the girl replied. "There isn't a single plastic cover on any of the furniture."

Hamish wasn't bowled over by her reasoning, but at least they didn't have to worry about the broken window and lawyers.

Because it was daylight, the children were able to find their way home. Their parents were sleeping late like they used to when the kids stayed with Aunt Gertie and hadn't noticed the children were gone. Annoyed to be awakened, the woodcutter and his wife forgave the children when Hamish and Gretel took them to the cottage in the woods. They would have enough to eat for months, and even better, the trees here were plentiful. If they moved in, the woodcutter was sure he could write it off as a business expense.

The family lived there, and Aunt Gertie—who loved *halvah* and heard it was plentiful—even came to visit. She remembered Hamish and Gretel in her will after all, and so, finally, everyone lived happily ever after.

The Three Billy Goats Kosher

Once upon a time, Stan Beteavon and Sons ran a kosher farm where they also trained those who wished to learn the ways of preparing food according to Jewish dietary laws.

"Always remember," Stan would tell his class, "you can tell an animal is kosher if its hooves are completely parted at the bottom to form two horny pads and if it chews the cud.

"Pigs have split hooves but do not chew their cud, so they are not kosher. Also camels, though they chew their cud, have only partially split hooves, so they are also not kosher."

While no Jew in the tristate region was expected to encounter a camel except in reverie about multiple handmaidens and a visit to their tent, the students were told that cows, sheep, deer, and goats possessed both of these qualities and so were kosher.

Now overhearing this, a billy goat family by the

name of Gruff was no longer inclined to remain at the new home to which they had recently relocated.

"Live like the Bordens my *pipek*," grumped Papa Gruff.

He had been told by a crab at the beach—old Morty Levitch, the real estate *shnorrer*—that prices were slashed in this region. He had said nothing about gullets.

Chewing through the rope that bound him to a rail, Papa Gruff freed his wife and young son and led them out across the fields.

"Where will we go?" Mama Gruff wailed.

"Are we there yet?" Tiny Gruff asked.

"We must be patient," Papa Gruff replied with Solomonic solemnity. "We are now Wandering Jews."

"Not this *balhabusteh*," Mama Gruff shot back with annoyance. "You live in diaspora. I'm going to Miami."

And so it was decided. First, however, the Three Billy Goats Gruff had to get away from the Beteavons.

Upon reaching the old wooden bridge that forded the cascading stream at the edge of the property, they were about to go across when a man jumped out. He had eyes as big as saucers and a nose as long as a poker.

"Is it a troll?" cried Tiny Gruff.

"Hush, it's Abraham the Butcher," Papa Gruff replied, embarrassed because his son knew not from goiters.

Having noticed that they were gone, Abraham informed the Beteavons that he was off to get their goats and had taken a shortcut to beat them to the bridge. He had an order to fill for the Tinklemans, and these three were part of it.

Papa and Mama Gruff hid behind a tree while urging their son ahead. He was a little *nudnik*. He'd find a way to cross.

Trip, trap, trip, trap, trip, trap came the sound from ahead.

"Who's that tripping over my bridge?" roared Abraham, his cleaver raised high. "It is only I," Tiny Gruff replied, "and I'm going up to the hillside to make myself fat."

"Oh?" asked Abraham, thinking that was not such a bad idea—but still suspicious of this *pisher*. "Why would you do that?"

Then the youngest Gruff raised and dropped his little shoulders and asked a question no Jew can answer: "Why not?"

"All right," Abraham said, thinking this *pitzel* wouldn't be good for more than a few dishes of spread. "You can go ahead."

Thanking the butcher, Tiny Gruff skipped across the bridge as if he hadn't a care in the world, which he didn't. Ever since the billy goats changed their name from Gruphsky, the rams had stopped pulling his beard, so things were pretty good.

Next, Papa Gruff urged his wife to approach the bridge.

Trip, trap, trip, trap, trip, trap went her garishly polished hooves on the bridge.

"Who's that tripping over my bridge?" roared Abraham.

"It's Mama Gruff," she replied, "and I'm going up to the hillside to make myself fat."

"You're already one *zoftig* nanny goat," Abraham said.

"I believe your condition has affected your eyesight," she replied thickly, when what she really wanted to do was kick him right in his phylacteries. "I am actually considered quite svelte."

"By whom, Nahum the Astigmatic?"

"By my husband, Papa Gruff, who will be along shortly." Mama Gruff huffed.

"Go back to the farm," Abraham ordered.

Instead, the billy goat stepped forward conspiratorially. "Truthfully? He's much, much bigger than I am. He's all you'll need to take care of the Tinkle-man party."

"You know about that?" Abraham asked.

"The cows talk," she admitted.

"Goat *in Himmel!*" Abraham cried. "All right, you may pass. But don't make me come up there," he indicated the hills with his cleaver.

"I promise, you will not have to chase us," she replied with a knowing nod that made Abraham uneasy.

With that, Mama Gruff sauntered by.

Papa Gruff didn't know whether to be proud of his wife for getting past or troubled that she was ready to offer him up like Isaac on the altar. As he stepped from behind the tree, he began to wonder—as he often did—how life would have been different had he married LaToya, an ibex who had a sweet disposition and horns to die for. But she was from Africa and such a thing just wasn't done.

A *nechtiker tog*, he thought as he approached Abraham with a trip, trap, trip, trap, trip, trap.

"Who's that tripping over my bridge?" roared Abraham.

"It is I, Papa Gruff!" said the billy goat. "I've come to collect my wife!" He added, shouting, "my *behaimeh* of a wife!"

Papa Gruff saw her look back with a *punim* like his mother had made when he told her about LaToya.

"I've let her and your son go to the hill to graze," Abraham said. "But you will not escape, goat. You must come back with me to the—"

That was the last thing Papa Gruff heard as Abraham's voice was swallowed by the clomp of hooves and his own hoarse scream. Abraham was struck from behind by Mama Gruff, who sent him *tuchas* over teakettle off the bridge and into the stream that carried him off.

Papa Gruff used to tease Mama about her "big butt" but it was no joke. Neither was her expression.

"A *behaimeh*?" Mama Gruff shouted as she approached her husband. "A *behaimeh*? Is that what I am?"

Papa Gruff replied with a little smile, "Gnu?"

Mama Gruff stood there for a moment, snorting. Then she huffed, half turned, and grinned.

"*Shmegegi,*" she said.

Mama Gruff remembered at that moment why she had married Papa Gruff. He wasn't handsome or a *macher,* but he was a *mensch* with a sense of humor.

"*Nu, shoyn!,*" she answered back, and as she had suggested, the Three Billy Goats Gruff set off across the bridge, up and over the hillside, and eventually reached Miami where they all got so fat and tan that they were indistinguishable from the other transplants.

Except that more often than not, through their many years together, Mama and Papa Gruff could be heard laughing about something or other.

Snow Whitefish and the Seven Dwarfkins

ears ago, in the part of New York City that wasn't an island—the Bronx—Snow Whitefish felt as though she herself was an island. And not a nice one like the Bahamas, but Cuba or Haiti or one of those *hekdish* places. While the other girls went to secretarial school in the hopes of going to work for—and maybe even landing, they could hope—a nice CPA or attorney, poor Snow Whitefish was forced to work for her stepmother Queenie Whitefish, the caterer.

Queenie's own two daughters attended Yalda University where they typed, took dictation, and also gave it.

"I can't afford help, and your father is a *foiler* who sleeps all day," embittered Queenie Whitefish said.

In truth, Kaiser Whitefish had been in mourning for years, ever since his wife Sophie had choked on a large piece of not-so-chopped herring from Queenie's shop. The caterer avoided a lawsuit—and gained a free worker—by marrying Kaiser in his *farmisht* frame of mind.

The long hours and Queenie's cruelty made life difficult for young Snow, especially when young men would come calling. Snow was particularly fond of Sam Prince, a dentist who came each day for the *knaidlech*.

One day, not long before Hanukkah, but after first arguing how to spell it on the sign in the window, the women fought about how to prepare the potatoes for *latkes*.

"It's not efficient to shred," Snow told her stepmother. "You could make more if you blended."

"It is not pure to purée," Queenie snapped back. "Keep peeling."

Disgusted, Snow not only left the shop but she left the Bronx, taking a bus to Forest Hills. It was night when she arrived, and being unfamiliar with the area and having no money, she walked through Flushing Meadows until exhaustion overtook her. She curled up beside a fence made of chain link, which felt to her back like the terrible mattress at home, one on which Queenie's daughters had bounced so often with suitors that the spring was gone.

It was well after midnight when the beam of a

flashlight fell upon the sleeping form of Snow Whitefish.

"A Jewish woman camping!" marveled Noshy Dwarfkin, one of the Dwarfkin Furriers who owned the property on the other side of the fence. Still chewing on a drumstick, he immediately ran to get his six brothers.

"For this you woke me?" chastised Kvetchy Dwarfkin, rubbing his squinty eyes.

"Sh-sh-she's n-n-not from around here," grinned Funfeh Dwarfkin, pulling his trench coat tight though it was an unusually warm, clear night.

"Whoever she is, we shouldn't get involved," suggested Parshiveh Dwarfkin.

"I like her outfit," remarked Tsitskeh Dwarfkin, whose dream was to join Hadassah and wear furs, not just around the house.

Fortzy Dwarfkin made no comment, though the fragrance of the air attested to his enthusiasm.

"She be fine, so take her in," rapped the seventh and youngest brother, Shaquille, who was also swarthier and much taller than his brethren were and whose arrival into the household had caused a rift between Mr. and Mrs. Dwarfkin that resulted in loud recriminations and ended with Mrs. Dwarfkin taking to her sickbed, never to recover. It also resulted in

Mr. Dwarfkin taking to the bed of Miss Parkchester before joining her in Hollywood where he knew people who could help her career, which is how his sons came to have the fur business.

Now all this chatter had caused Snow Whitefish to stir. Since the first thing she saw was Shaquille coming over the fence, she screamed and was instantly on her feet, fumbling in her purse for the mace that her father had wisely suggested she carry. Fortunately, the other six Dwarfkins followed close behind and stopped her from *shpritzing*.

"You must not blind a brother!" Noshy cautioned her, wagging the drumstick.

"O-o-our brother," Funfeh clarified.

"Your brother?" Snow Whitefish said, not quite sure she was awake.

Nonetheless, feeling unthreatened by Jews, she followed the *farkuckt* little men into the compound. Upon entering the warehouse, the young woman thought she had died and gone to Bergdorf Goodman.

Furs were everywhere, racks and racks of coats and stoles and accessories like hats and gloves.

Snow shuddered in a most delightful and unfamiliar manner, drawing unwanted winks and grins from Shaquille.

"Yo, you be high, ho!" he said in a singsong voice.

"I'm wishing you'd get lost, *farshtaist*?"

"I dig, dig, dig," he answered.

Upon composing herself—unlike those songs—Snow hurried to catch up to the others.

"Do you people make all of these?" she asked Kvetchy.

"No, they make themselves," he sneered. "Of course we make them."

"*We are the Dwarfkin furriers!*" shouted Fortzy, for he was well behind the others.

"I have often gazed with longing upon your wares in the paper and in stores," Snow said. "But they should not be shown on mannequins."

"Dummies are not so expensive," remarked Parshiveh with a shrug of his bony shoulders.

"Then I will model your furs," offered Snow.

"For how much?" Parshiveh asked suspiciously.

"I will charge you nothing but your hospitality."

This was a deal the Dwarfkins could not refuse, for it was coming upon the gift-giving season, and they needed to compete with the Kakamuni Brothers who used exotic Asian models and deep discounts to attract customers to their Korean-made products.

Tsitskeh took photographs of Snow wearing a variety of furs, which they planned to advertise in the

Forward, as always. However, Snow convinced them to go a little wider so they also took space in several New York papers, but without telling Parshiveh.

Meanwhile, working night and day to fill orders, Queenie Whitefish took a moment to check her own quarter-page advertisement in the *Daily Mirror.* As she did, her skin went as white as her namesake, for what should she see on that same page but an ad for Dwarfkins' Furs promising prices that were *the fairest in the land, unless you want cheap imports.* Yet that was not the worst of it, for who did she see modeling a coat but her own ungrateful stepdaughter!

Queenie shrieked and threw the newspaper so hard that it stuck to the greasy tiles behind the oven.

"I'll give you *fair!*" she screamed, glaring at the mirror on the wall. "I'll give you my bill of fare!"

Unaware of her wicked stepmother's latest *mishe-gas,* Snow was busy celebrating a big jump in sales with the Dwarfkins. They were preparing to order in from Mama Buddha and watch reruns of *Seinfeld.* As Kvetchy called the restaurant, there was suddenly a knock at the door. Shaquille answered, having ordered something for himself and expecting her to arrive about now.

"Bizzo, I hope you ain't Lolita Kwan," he said.

"I am Tillie Opnarer," she cackled. The visitor

was a hunched woman, wearing a hood and covering her age spots with flour. "Would any of you care for *latkes*?"

Thinking she recognized the voice, Snow came to the door. There, a figure like a *dybbuk* held a plate covered with tin foil.

"I am Snow Whitefish," she said. "Do I know you?"

"Daughter of Sophie Whitefish?"

Snow nodded.

"I used to play Canasta with your mother," the woman replied as she extended the plate.

"Will you take them? I made too many and I hate for them to go to waste."

"I shouldn't," Snow replied. "We're ordering Chinese."

"You deny me this *mitzvah*?" the woman guilted her. "I would like to see you lick your fingers the way Sophela would lick her thumb when she dealt— a disgusting habit—and who might still be alive if she spent less time *shpaying* and more time chewing her herring."

Snow was more annoyed than touched, but she knew that the only way to get rid of a *yenta* was to do what she asked. Lifting the edge of the tin foil, she broke off a piece of *latke*—it was cold—and placed it between lips that were still painted from the photo shoot, which made her look cheap, Queenie thought.

"Mmmmm," Snow said as she chewed, quickly licking her fingers and hoping the lady would leave now so she could spit into a napkin.

But the visitor just stood in the doorway, noticing the cheap *mezuzah* from the corner of her eye and then watching with *nachas* as Snow swooned and dropped to the floor.

"Snow fall!" Funfeh yelled ungrammatically.

"*Gai kucken ahfen yam!*" Queenie cried, throwing off her wrap and standing upright. "You will soon be with your mother, for there was pork in that *latke!*"

With that, Queenie ran into the night, leaving her stepdaughter unconscious and six of the Dwarfkins in mourning, Shaquille having gone upstairs when his date showed up during all the *haken a tsheinik*.

Yet Queenie was not the only one to have seen the Dwarfkin ad, for who should arrive within minutes but the dentist Sam Prince, who had recognized Snow's picture and came to ask for a discount on a fur for his mother.

Being led to the rug where they'd plopped her, for the Dwarfkins weren't strong like Samson but flimsy like *lokshen*, Prince noticed a strand of *latke* in her teeth.

"The *latke* was shredded, not puréed," he said. "The *traif* may yet be in her teeth!"

Pulling out the floss he carried at all times, the dentist quickly but firmly cleaned between every tooth in her mouth until he found the offending meat. Upon its removal, the eyes of Snow Whitefish fluttered and opened and met those of Dr. Prince.

"I owe you my life," she said.

"True," he said modestly, "but I will settle for a fur at a little below wholesale."

And that was how Dr. Prince came to give his mother a nice mink coat for Hanukkah and how Snow came to be invited to the Prince family home for dinner where she met his brother Larry, who was only an accountant but whom she married for at least he showed her some interest.

As for Queenie, the mirror on the wall caught fire when she lit the oven, and her place of business burned down. She perished in that blaze, but her husband hit the jackpot because he collected insurance on both the building and his wife.

Larry became Kaiser's accountant and grew his fortune greatly. Snow continued to model for the Dwarfkins and everyone was happy—even Shaquille, who married Lolita and took over her business, for he already had the clothes; and Tsitskeh Dwarfkin, who entered into a civil union with Dr. Prince.

"*Gloib mir*, this is after all a fairy tale!" Kvetchy noted.

Pushkin Boots

nce there was a Muscovite tailor whose only inheritance to his three sons was his shop, his tools, and his cat Pushkin, named after the author of *Boris Godunov*, for what Jew could fail to love this story of an anti-Semite who killed a tsar, became a tsar, and died a *manzer*?

When the tailor passed on, the eldest took the shop; the second the needles, thread, and fabric; and the youngest the cat.

Young Lester, realizing he'd been screwed by that *nochshlepper* attorney Sammy Fox, who wrote the will—and brought nothing to the *shiva*, yet ate all the *kugel*—said to his elder brothers, "I'm no *maiven*, but it seems to me we could make a handsome living by joining our shares, no?"

"No!" they said as one, chuckling at both the wordplay and his naiveté.

Meantime, the cat, who heard all this, went over and whispered in his master's ear, "If you will but give me a bag and a nice pair of boots—leather, like that Russian boy had in *Fiddler*, not cloth like the Jews—then you shall see you are not so poorly off with me as you think!"

Lester looked at the cat, amazed. "How is it that you speak?"

"I am Reform Mewish," Pushkin explained.

Now the youngest brother had often seen Pushkin play cunning tricks to catch rats, so he got the cat what he'd asked for at the reading of the will.

"What are you going to do?" Lester asked, intrigued.

"Make the tsar our *lantsman*," he said.

"*Kain ein horeh!*" wailed the youth. "I have a cat who can talk, but he is *meshugeh*!"

"*Meshugeh* like a Sammy Fox," Pushkin said before setting out.

Heading directly to a place where there were many rabbits, Pushkin opened his bag, which contained carrots. Then he stretched himself out as if he were dead. Soon, a foolish young hare jumped into the bag, and the cat quickly tied it shut. Then he went to the palace and, with a low bow, presented the rabbit to the tsar with the compliments of his master.

"Who is your master?" the tsar asked.

"The great merchant Ivory," Pushkin replied.

"I know not your master, but I thank him for this gift," said the tsar.

Before leaving, Pushkin rubbed his tiny paws, for the boots had not been broken in. As he massaged his paw, he took careful note of the activities of everyone at the palace, especially the grooms.

Returning to his master, Pushkin said, "If you follow my advice tomorrow, your fortune will be made."

"Wonderful," Lester said, "for all I have made today is a *greps*. What are we to do?"

The cat told Lester that he must go to the river and bathe early the next morning.

The boy did as he was told, hoping none of the village girls came by, for the water was cold and his *baitsim* were shriveled. Suddenly, he heard the cat yelling.

"Help! Help!" Pushkin cried.

Looking out at the commotion, Lester saw the coach of the tsar rumbling toward him. Quickly, the boy ducked down so that he would not be connected with a cat that was so obviously mad. This was exactly what Pushkin knew he would do.

"Will no one help my master?" yelled the cat. "Can't you see he is drowning?"

Recognizing the cat, the tsar commanded his guards to help the young man. While they were so engaged, the cat cried out again.

"*Shmatta* thieves!" he yelled, pointing to the far banks.

In fact, there were no robbers. The cat had hidden Lester's clothes behind a tree.

The tsar immediately commanded other of his men to return to the palace and fetch a suit for the young man, one worthy of his status.

Upon being finely accoutered, Lester came forth, whereupon the tsar's daughter noticed him and immediately took a liking to him. The tsar saw this and asked Lester to enter the coach and join them on their constitutional. Though it pained Lester to accept the hospitality of such a renowned oppressor, his eyes were on the tsaritza who had quite a *knish* in her lap.

Pleased at the progress of his plan, the cat ran ahead to the docks where he knew the tsar's path must take them. He approached the foreman of the wharf.

"If you do not say that this cargo belongs to the merchant Ivory, I shall gouge out your eyes," Pushkin threatened.

"You and what army?" the burly worker challenged.

"His," said the cat, jerking a claw toward the royal carriage of the tsar.

The dockworker absently tugged on an oarlock and agreed to do as Pushkin had asked.

As the carriage approached, the tsar saw the itinerant cat standing on a crate talking to the dockworker.

"And these crates are all the property of my master?" the cat asked.

"Every last one," replied the dockworker.

"*Loch in kop!*" Pushkin said with a sigh. "We'll have to send extra *shtarkers* to move them so great a distance to our warehouse in Kiev."

The tsar was indeed impressed and asked the young man if he cared to wait at the palace while the workers were found to take care of the cargo. Lester was still uneasy until the tsaritza offered him a taste of her *knish*.

Lester accepted, tickled by how many pussies there could be in just one short tale.

It wasn't long before the tsaritza and the closeted Jew were wed with great celebration, to which Lester's family was not invited—though they received a photo album as a little *kush mein tuchas*.

As for Pushkin, he became a great tsarevich and never again ran after mice, though he did chase the occasional *tallis* fringe, just to blend in.

Rumpleforeskin

Once there was a miller—Irving Miller—who was poor but who had a beautiful daughter, Fern, the result of marrying outside the faith. Now it happened that Irving had to go and speak to the rabbi about an order of grain for Pesach *matzohs*. In order to make himself appear important, Irving said to him, "*Rebbe* Nehemiah, I have a daughter who can spin straw into gold. And not the 14K *ongepatcheket* that Mrs. Birnbaum wears on her fleshy wrists, either."

The rabbi said to Miller, "That is an art which pleases me, and my son Isaac who is lazy will never earn a living. If your daughter is as clever as you say, bring her tomorrow to *shul* and I will put her to the test."

Oy, thought Irving, who could just as well have promised to grow silver *payas* for all the gold spinning his daughter Fern could actually perform.

When the girl was brought to him, the rabbi took

her into a closet that was full of boxes of the Mendel wedding *yarmulkes* and was also quite full of straw. He gave her a spinning wheel and told her to get to work.

"If by tomorrow morning you have not spun this straw into gold, you must cook breakfast for the entire *minyan*. The way Yankel eats, you will be here all day." Whereupon he locked her in the closet and left her in it alone.

"There is *shmutz* here!" she yelled after looking around, but her words went unheeded.

So there sat poor Fern Miller, and for the life of her, she had no idea what to do except to whine. She whined and whined until at last she began to complain about the room being stuffy and, now that she thought of it, ripe with whatever Isaac had been doing with the Greenbergs' daughter when they arrived.

All at once she heard a stirring, then saw a little man—one who was even shorter than Old Malachi the Hem Alterer.

This man said, "Good day, Mistress Miller. Why does the young Jewess whine so—or is that redundant?"

She smacked him and then said, "I have to spin

straw into gold, and I do not know how to do it. Also—how did you get in here?"

"I fell asleep under the Mel Gibson DVDs, which are being returned," he replied. "So what will you give me if I do it for you?"

"Are you of the faith?"

"I am."

"Good," she said. "Then you will want riches instead of my honor. I'll tell you what. You may have my gold necklace."

"That will get you a *schmeck und leck*," he said.

The little man took the necklace and, after making sure it wasn't just plate, seated himself in front of the wheel. After a whirr, whirr, whirr—just three turns—the reel was full of gold.

"*Ut azoy!*" proclaimed the little man.

"Very nice," Fern said. "Okay. How much to turn all the straw into gold?"

"*Vey is mire,*" he muttered. "So doing, you will marry the rabbi's son?"

"I will."

"And if I help, you will wear a gown designed by my sister Rose?"

"Rose the Stripper?"

"She wants to get out of the business," said the little man.

"What choice do I have?" Fern sighed. "It's a bargain."

The magical *homunculus* went to work. By morning, the straw had all been turned into gold, and Fern Miller was about to become Mrs. Isaac Nebech.

Unfortunately, after catching Rose's act on Cable Access, Fern had a change of heart. When she complained to her tiny *messiah*, he took pity on her—and was also eager for her to stop talking so loud. And fast. And overmuch.

"Tell you what," he said. "As it is soon to be the Sabbath, I will give you three days. If by that time you find out my name, then you can go to Vera Wang with my blessings."

She thought the whole night of all the names that she had ever heard and also sent a Sabbath *Goy* over the country to inquire, far and wide, for any other names that there might be.

When the little man came the next day, she began with Abraham, Saul, David, Moses, and Charlton and said all the Jewish names she knew, one after another. But to every one the wee one said, "Not even warm!"

The second day was equally unprofitable, as she started with Ron Jeremy whom he much resembled and moved on to the names of closeted Jews.

"Shatner? Bacall? Winkler?"

"*Nyet!*" he chortled.

On the third day the Sabbath *Goy* said, "I have not been able to find a single new name, but as I came to a nice place, nothing fancy—but with a terrace—I saw a man jumping and drinking a nice French kosher wine as he shouted:

> *Today I bake, tomorrow brew,*
> *My sister soon won't bother this Hebrew!*
> *Ha, glad am I that no one knew*
> *That Rumpleforeskin I am, the Jew!*

You may imagine how glad the almost-woman was when she heard the name. When soon afterwards the *nebbish* came in, Fern folded her arms, and the fellow knew he was in for it.

"*Nu*, Rumpleforeskin?" she said.

"The devil has told you that!" he cried.

"No," she said. "Juan the gardener."

In a rage, Rumpleforeskin plunged his right foot so deep into the earth that his whole leg went in, and then in worse rage, he pulled at his left leg so hard with both hands that he tore himself in two—right where his foreskin was, revealing him to have been an imposter on top of everything else.

Fern fed him to the cats, so it shouldn't be a total waste.

The Ugly Shmuckling

For years, Mrs. Esther Duchovny had been bringing her four sons to sit with her by the pool at a Jewish Community Center in Long Island, Nassau County, which was rich with Jews who were not so wealthy that they could go to the Hamptons for a weekend or, God willing, the entire summer.

But her youngest and most *nebbishy* boy, Joseph, did not like to get wet or put on a swimsuit or even talk to other members of the JCC who sat on chaise longues sipping sodas, even though they weren't supposed to bring them so close to the pool.

"*Tatteleh*," Esther said one day, "you're seventeen. You should find yourself a friend."

"Ma, I'm busy," he said without looking from his laptop. He continued to read from a website called From Judas to You, about famous and successful Jewish men, such as Max Linder, who had taken their own lives.

"You should at least wash," Esther suggested. "With all this sun you're a little *farshtunken*."

"I don't want to go anywhere," he replied. "This is a hot spot."

"Isn't that what I just said?" she asked.

Joseph didn't bother to explain.

She glanced toward a woman who was sitting in the shade. "I hear that Alma Feingold's daughter Suzy is going to be stopping by later to pick up her mother."

"Then you can take her place under the tree."

"Don't be smart," Esther said, looking at her hands and turning the rings so they faced the same way, for they had slipped due to perspiration. "It wouldn't hurt for you to meet this daughter."

"Fine."

"Feingold," Esther said. "I hear she's very pretty. You know, not every boy has to have a clear complexion and a *pitsvinik* little nose like Jude Law and eyebrows plucked in the center—"

"Ma!" he snapped.

Esther raised her hands in surrender and then laid them with a heavy slap upon her thighs, which rippled as though a toad had jumped in marsh water.

Joseph continued to read about Max Linder while his mother continued to talk, only now to the long gone *Rebbe* Edelman whom she had always asked for guidance. It was thought among many that Mrs. Duchovny's fondness for *schnapps* and speed dialing were what drove him to seek reassignment, reportedly in the Third World.

Soon the mother and son were joined by Joseph's other brothers, all of whom were laughing and bronzed and wearing Speedos that their grandmother called *tuchas derma*, so tight were they. Their joy made Mrs. Duchovny both happy and *tsetumult* and made her regret all the more that her youngest was not like them.

"*Bubelehs*, come!" Esther announced suddenly. "I have a job for all of you!"

Though some of the boys rolled their eyes, they followed their mother, once two of them had helped her from the chair. Joseph didn't move.

"You too," she said sternly.

"Why?"

She gave the one answer no Jewish boy could refuse: "Because I said so."

Joseph did not bother speaking to *Rebbe* Edelman but spoke directly to God, asking for His help. As he did, Joseph put the laptop under a towel so that it shouldn't take direct sun or be seen by one of the lifeguards, who were not of the faith and therefore not to be trusted—according to his mother—even though every day it was the Jews who tried to *shtup* their father the zipper salesman on the corner of 36th and Seventh, which Isaac Duchovny had called the no-fly zone before the Arabs got it.

Her back marked with Jewish lashings—impressions from the beach chair—and her suit so damp it could not have gotten that wet swimming, Esther took the boys to the outdoor shower, which no one ever used because the water was too cold.

"Show Joseph how to wash off!" she said, continuing on so her boys would rinse and hurry after her.

One by one the brothers Duchovny walked through the water, tugging the rusted iron chain and shivering as they passed beneath the misty *shpritz*—which, ironically, was the name of a star discovered by the renowned Jewish pornographer Irving Craw, who knew he had a weak heart yet spent a weekend with his star and perished, inspiring the coroner to call it a suicide.

When it was Joseph's turn, he was actually grateful for the cold spray, thoughts of Misty having occupied him as he waited his turn. It was either that or look at his mother, the spread of whose thighs had bested the elasticity of her one-piece.

After her youngest had finished, the train of *kinderlech* moved on to the snack bar. There she said, "Boys—teach your brother how to dine like a proper Jew so that he may afford a date."

The young men did as they were told, each ordering a mushroom *knish* but taking a thick stack of napkins and straws along with much ketchup, mustard, relish, salt, pepper, Sweet'N Low, and regular sugar for the *shmegegis* who still thought the substitutes caused cancer and yet drank Diet Coke. Upon leaving, the boys also explained to Joseph what they had learned from their father: how Priority Mail envelopes, free from the post office, made very good file folders.

Their next stop was the locker room, which Joseph had always called the *locher* room, for to him it had all the appeal of a big, smelly hole.

"Take your brother and see that he puts on his trunks!" Esther commanded.

The young men didn't protest. There was no point, since their mother barred the way like a *golem*.

Joseph and his brethren entered the tiled chamber, their footsteps echoing like it was the reform *shul* on any day but Yom Kippur. The young man was resigned to tucking himself into tight mesh instead of the boxers, which allowed his *baitsim* to breathe as God had intended before Eve got off her *keister* and made a *tsimmes*.

Under the watchful eyes of his brothers, Joseph changed into the tight-fitting garment and donned loose-fitting flip-flops that nonetheless cut the flesh beside his big toe. When he was done, the other boys stood back.

"Mama will be pleased," said one.

"As pleased as mama can be," said another, cautioning as ever against optimism.

"I've got to pee," announced Joseph. "I'll come to the pool in a minute."

"You promise?" asked the eldest. "She'll come in here to get you—"

"I know," he said, remembering an incident in elementary school when his mother had entered the boy's room and pulled him out by the ear because he had made Joan Berger cry on the school bus by calling her "Joan Hamburger," even though that *kochleffel* Fred Frankfurter had told him that was her real name. "I'll be there."

The truth was, Joseph didn't have to pee. He left by another door and walked to the front of the com-

munity center where there were benches. He sat on one, not far from where a *shaineh maidel* was sitting.

"Are you hiding too?" the pretty girl asked.

Joseph nodded.

"Why?" she asked.

"My mother wants me to meet someone," he answered.

"And you don't want to."

Joseph nodded again.

"What would you rather be doing?" she asked.

He told her he had been reading about Max Linder, and then a miraculous thing occurred.

"You mean the silent French film star?" she asked.

Joseph's dark eyes lit up. "You've heard of him?" he cried, it having been his experience that what Jewish women knew of cinema or comedy could fill a *pipek*.

"I hope to study film at NYU," she told him. "I want to be a screenwriter."

"What is your name?" Joseph asked, awestruck.

"Suzy Feingold," she replied. "And I think you're cuter than my old boyfriend Fred Frankfurter."

Boldly taking her hand and singing "Miracle of Miracles" as he ran back to the swimming pool, Joseph had gone from being Motel Kamzoil to feeling like the movie star Jeff Chandler, who did not die by his own violent hand but from blood poisoning due to medical malpractice.

As his mother both enjoyed and suffered *chaloshes* and the other women fanned her, Joseph leaped into the pool and cried joyfully from the depths of his heart, "I never dreamed of such happiness all the while I was an ugly *shmuckling*!"

The Torah Rebbe and
the Hare Krishna

here once was a very tall and speedy Hindu named Ganesh who, between solicitations, bragged about how fast he could pray.

"I can recite the Veda faster than any swami," he said to anyone who would listen.

This being Miami, a block from the Chabad Institute, few did.

However, one person heard him each and every morning as he made his way to the Institute and that was *Rebbe* Shlomo Chelmow, a hunched little man who shuffled along on eighty-year-old feet.

"You *barimer*," *Rebbe* Chelmow said, breaking his perennial silence one bright morning.

"That is Brahman, kindest sir," the Hindu replied.

Rebbe Chelmow stopped suddenly—something dangerous in a man his age, for he could break a rib.

He turned his wizened face toward the youthful, innocent eyes of the Hindu.

"You say to everyone who passes, 'Look at me pray! I'm so fast!'" *Rebbe* Chelmow complained. "It's enough to make a person crazy."

"Not to do so would make me crazy," the Hindu replied. "I pray fast that I may get home to my bride and engage in the tantric arts, which must be done slowly."

"Fast, slow, it's enough to make you *fartshadikt!*" *Rebbe* Chelmow said, holding his ears in mock pain.

"Do you not pray slowly and then *fast*?" the Hindu asked, chuckling at his own joke.

"*Hert zich ein!*" the *rebbe* said as he scolded the youth with a white and wrinkled finger. "It is not good to pray as you do. Words can get lost, meanings confused."

"Ah," said the Hindu, "but that is the advantage of having many gods! They all listen and so nothing is missed."

If the elderly *rebbe*'s hair and beard had not been white, they would have turned so right then. His eyes went wide like Sam Jaffe—not in *Gunga Din* but later, when he played Jews, before Dr. Zorba—and he said to the Hindu, "You are the bearer of *tsimmes*—"

"No sir, I am a yogi bearer—," the Hindu admitted, happy to swing at the easy ones.

"But I am determined to stop you from making everyone else in this neighborhood *farkuckt*," the *rebbe* went on. "I challenge you to a contest."

"What kind?"

"You will pray beside me."

"Gladly," the Hindu said graciously. "To what end?"

"To the end of our prayer books," said the *rebbe*, who was not himself above a bad pun. "You will go to the last Upanishad and I through the Torah. The loser agrees to go to another place—Boca, which is already crowded but *az och un vai.*"

"A wonderful idea!" cried the Hindu, dancing and rattling his tambourine to show his joy.

"And they call us *meshugeh*," thought the old Jew, who rarely did more than shake his finger as he had done.

The men agreed to meet the following morning on the beach, where quite a crowd had gathered to witness the match. It was not exactly a balanced crowd, with old Jewish men and women on deck chairs surrounded by chanting Hare Krishnas.

"But who said life was fair?" the *rebbe* thought, as

he did so often, at least three or four times every hour.

Taking his place beside the Hindu, *Rebbe* Chelmow assumed the traditional prayer position: slump-shouldered, bent-kneed, bowed head. Their backs to the sea, the men waited for the prearranged signal—Mr. Cohen coughing up phlegm—and the race began!

The Hindu dove into the Rigveda, the Sanskrit hymns, while the *rebbe davened* where any *foigel* should know to start: "In the beginning . . ."

As the crowd looked on—except for Mr. Lipshitz, who fell asleep, and Mrs. Horowitz who had bridge, who were both replaced by airport Hare Krishnas from whence the Salvation Army had chased them in an uneven contest—the Hindu tore into the Samavida while *Rebbe* Chelmow was still going on about Cain and Abel.

After finishing two of the four texts in his holy book, the Hindu was distracted by a group of tourists. Laying the text aside—for he was already up to Yajurveda while the *rebbe* was still swimming through the flood of Genesis—he approached them to extol the virtues of consciousness raising as taught by Bhaktivedanta Prabhupada.

Just saying the swami's name gave *Rebbe* Chelmow time to reach Exodus.

After driving the tourists off, the Hindu intended to return to his book. However, after an hour of celebrating, the energies of his fellow Krishnas seemed to flag. Thus, he joined them in revelry, his bald head shining with sweat.

"Such *kvitching!*" the *rebbe* thought, but he did not let it break his recitation. Moses freed the Jews from bondage while the *rebbe*'s rival carried on.

"Hare Krishna Hare Krishna Krishna Krishna Hare Rama . . ."

"What are they saying?" Mrs. Finkelstein asked no one in particular, as Jewish senior citizens are wont to do.

Hearing her, the Hindu went over and explained, "Hare refers to Lord Krishna's personal pleasure potency—"

"*Gotteniu!*" Mrs. Finkelstein cried as she hyperventilated.

"And Krishna describes the all-attractive and desirable lord!"

Mrs. Finkelstein keeled over. While the Hindu fanned the prostrate woman with the hem of his saffron sari, he went on, "As for Rama, that is the source of all enjoyment!"

Mrs. Finkelstein passed out, not from hearing

these words, but from the very idea that a human being should suffer from *enjoyment*.

By this time the *rebbe* was well into Leviticus and bearing down on Numbers.

The Hindu stood after praying for Mrs. Finkelstein, who seemed to be recovering. Because he had become sweaty from dancing on the beach, he went to the sea for a ritual cleansing. He returned just in time to hear a mantra his fellow Krishnas had composed to urge him to victory:

> *Two, four, six, eight—karma is our word for fate!*
> *One, three, five, seven—dharma is the way to heaven!*

Moved to tears, the Hindu hugged each and every one of his brethren before returning to the Veda. As he picked up his tome, he heard: "That Moses exhibited in the sight of all Israel. *Ohmain!*"

"Amen?" the Hindu repeated as he looked quizzically at the *rebbe*.

"You have done your duty, while I have done my Deuteronomy," *Rebbe* Chelmow announced with a rare smile that caused Mrs. Finkelstein to pass out anew.

"You're finished?" the Hindu asked in amazement.

"No," said the Talmudist. "I've won. You're finished!"

And so, as per their agreement, the Hindu—who was a *mensch* in defeat—agreed to go to Boca. The fellow was optimistic he would prosper, though if he only knew how many more Jews there were than in Miami, he might have decided to go to Salt Lake City instead.

As the *rebbe* told those who remained, the lesson of the contest is not that one religion is better than another, for such is not the case.

"The moral," he said, "is that slow and steady wins for our Race."

The Three Little
Chazzers

In a quiet little village in a great European forest, there lived a little old *challah* maker who fell upon hard times. All the villagers, even the Jews, suddenly seemed to want French bread, which he refused to make because—well, *French*.

"I would have made white bread, even *chazzer* rye, but not this," he said unhappily to his wife, as they counted out their dwindling savings.

Realizing that they could no longer support their three young sons, who ate a great deal and then some, the baker sent them out into the world.

"To seek your fortune," he told them, but it was really so that the old baker and his wife would have enough money at least to make French toast, which he liked despite the fact that—well, *French*.

Since the three young *chazzers* had neither wealth nor education nor anything approaching good looks, they stopped by the local money lender, the black-bearded Lenny Wolfowitz, and borrowed just enough at twelve percent to get started.

The youngest of the three brothers, who was also the laziest, bought a bundle of straw to build a house, for it was inexpensive and would leave him enough *gelt* to buy jam *chremslach* because he did not want to look for a job on an empty stomach. He did not want to look for a job at all, but his chances of finding a wealthy wife who was also blind were not so good.

The middle *chazzer* was a little less lazy and a little less cheap. He bought a bundle of sticks and put up a sturdier house of wood—like a *sukkot* but without the festive garlands.

The eldest *chazzer*, a Type-*Aleph* first born, was much more industrious. He too bought cheap straw and a little bit of wood. But he also used skills his ancestors had learned during servitude in Egypt to make little rectangular frames from the wood. He chopped the straw into pieces and dropped them into a mud pit, mixed it up with his feet, and then fashioned blocks, which he left to dry in the sun. When he had enough, this *chazzer* built a home from bricks.

While the older brother was hard at work, his younger siblings were being little *foilers*. They slept late, and when they woke, they sang and danced.

> *Enschultig meir Wolfowitz*
> *Wolfowitz*
> *Wolfowitz*
> *Enschultig meir Wolfowitz*
> *Drai mir nit kain kop!*

Naturally, the brothers composed an all-new melody for the words, even though they fit so nicely into a familiar air associated with this tale.

The song caught on among the many who owed money and quickly reached the ears of Lenny Wolfowitz. Fearful that the brothers' rebellious *k'nacking* would inspire others to stiff him, the usurer pulled on his fur coat and headed out to collect the debt.

It was late when he arrived at the nearest of the houses, the one made of straw. The youngest brother had already gone inside for the night.

Knocking on the door, Wolfowitz said, "Little *chazzer*, little *chazzer*, let me come in!"

His angry voice frightened the lad, triggering racial memory flashbacks to a Polish attic in 1939.

"No, not by the hair of my chinny chin chin!" the young *chazzer* replied.

"Who are you, Hymie the Stutterer?" he asked. "If you don't open the door I'll huff and I'll puff and I'll blow your house in!"

"*Kish mein tuchas!*" the *chazzer* replied with bravado, though his voice was trembling.

"I'll do that right before I sue!" the moneylender said.

Enraged now, he huffed and he puffed and he blew the straw house so hard that it flew away. It should come down sometime next year in Jerusalem.

Rather than wait for the ream—of paperwork—the terrified *chazzer* ran off in the direction of the middle brother's house. Feeling like a regular Samson, Wolfowitz pursued the welsher, tracking him by the pork-like smell of fear.

When he arrived at the wood house, for this was the littlest *chazzer*'s destination, Wolfowitz leaned close to the door and snarled, "Little *chazzer*, little *chazzer*, let me come in."

Not the *dumkop* his younger brother was, the

middle *chazzer* merely answered, "No, not by the hair of my chinny chin chin!"

"You would rather be in court for years?"

"We would rather you just charge us fourteen percent and go away, Shylock!" the younger *chazzer* squealed.

Though the offer of higher interest held his interest for a moment, the epithet made him snort.

"I'll puff and I'll huff and I'll blow your house in!" he raged.

And so he did. While this house put up a little more of a struggle, about like Lebanon, it fell before his windy wrath.

Even as splinters were flying like a plague of locusts, the two little *chazzers* were off and running to the brick *shtark* house of their brother. Not only would he protect them, they knew, but it was nearly dinnertime and he usually made soup.

Once again Lenny Wolfowitz followed, though a bit more slowly because, frankly, he felt more like Delilah now. He wasn't used to such exertion.

Still, it wasn't long before he arrived at the house of the third little *chazzer*. Once more he said, "Little *chazzer*, little *chazzer*, let me come in!"

"No, not by the hair of my chinny chin chin!" said the eldest brother.

"Again with that nonsense!" Wolfowitz said. "You know, you might want to reconsider. This is not covered by the homeowner's policy my brother Sid sold you."

"Stop talking and start blowing," the *chazzer* taunted, for an idea was occurring to him.

"*Hokay*," the moneylender warned. "I'll huff and I'll puff and I'll blow your house in!"

Well, the bearded Jew huffed and he puffed and he huffed and he puffed and he puffed and he huffed until the brick house seemed to spin like a *dreidel*. But no matter how hard he blew, he could not knock that house down.

This made Wolfowitz angry like a hornet—which is probably why he also thought he could fly, for he jumped and jumped and tried to get to an open window on the second floor.

"You'll never reach it!" taunted the youngest of the *chazzers*, repeating what the eldest had told him to say.

"No!" said the middle *chazzer* as he'd been told. "Why don't you try the chimney?"

"I think I will!" the moneylender said, flexing fingers that were strong from years of pinching *shekels*.

The two boys laughed and laughed as Wolfowitz went around back. As he thought, the bricks of the chimney were just a little bit soft from the heat of the fire in the hearth.

"They are not so frail that I can tear them down," he murmured, "but I can dig my fingers into them and climb!"

Which was exactly what the eldest *chazzer* expected him to do, after sending his *shmendrick* brothers to taunt him.

As Wolfowitz ascended, the third little *chazzer* poured chicken soup into the large kettle in the hearth. Then he put the lid on so Wolfowitz shouldn't smell it. Minutes later, as the moneylender was coming down the chimney, the eldest *chazzer* took off the cover. The steam caused the bricks to soften further and into the kettle fell Wolfowitz.

Badly burned, and with chicken chunks lodged deep from *moyel* to *pipek*, he was easily overcome by the *chazzers*. They kept him for the constable, who charged the moneylender with destruction of property and breaking and entering. The *chazzers* agreed to drop the charges in exchange for a clean financial slate. Forgiving their debt hurt Wolfowitz worse than the second-degree burns, but they had his *shvontz* in a vice.

As for the Three Little Chazzers, they prospered, for they had learned a valuable lesson: don't work too hard but *shnorr* off others.

The Jewish American Princess and the Pea

nce upon a time in New York City, there was a founding partner at Steinberg & Metz who wanted a wife to make the other lawyers jealous and enhance his status in Westchester. But finding one who was young, attractive, and Jewish was not easy! Sol Steinberg joined online dating services, lingered at Columbia University where he taught, and went to *shul* where he always seemed to find himself between middle-aged divorcées, who sapped his energies with talk of their children and how moving it had been to go to *Eretz* Israel—which they all pronounced Yees-row-ail as though they were *Sabras* and not *kishkes* in high heels.

Sol even sent matchmakers all over the world to locate a bride, yet nowhere could he find what he wanted.

Oh, they came back with videos of young women,

especially svelte young Russian girls, schooled in ways no Jewess would tolerate or even hear of without making a face. Yet these *tsatkehs* wanted a green card more than they desired a husband. It was difficult to find a true Jewish American Princess who didn't offend the eye if not the ear, would rather eat tasty than kosher, and could still be president of the Sisterhood.

The new associates at the firm—especially the young men whose wives wore pearls on their slender necks, wore headbands about their natural blonde tresses, and had surnames like Winters and Cook—were cheered by his futile efforts. It was their only distraction as they worked the long evening hours on the tedious gentile path to junior partnership.

All the while, Sol knew from sadness and loneliness which, no spring chicken at forty, he wished would end.

One afternoon, a probate case came to the firm. It was brought in by a young woman named Andrea—an education major at Hunter College, for she should have something to fall back on since she was so picky with men. Sol's JAP sister-in-law Ruth, who worked reception because it was something to do, noticed the raven-haired beauty at once and sent her to see

Sol. Even before being seated, the twenty-one-year-old complained to Sol that she was being denied access to her beloved Uncle Bernie's estate by the courts.

"Though I am his sole heir and not my cousin Fern who joined Jews for Jesus and was disowned, her attorneys say he has overseas accounts and until those are located nothing can be released," she sobbed to Sol without pausing for breath.

"Some process is necessary to transfer legal title of such items to the beneficiaries or heirs of the deceased," Sol informed her. "However, most states allow a limited amount of property to pass free of probate or through a greatly simplified probate procedure. We can discuss this further over a nice lunch."

Andrea's dark eyes flashed. She could scarcely still the racing heart beneath her blouse from Neiman Marcus, for this was just the kind of news she had wanted to hear about the money. She agreed to the meal, for even though Sol wasn't much to look at, neither were any of the *shmendricks* from Borough Park with whom her mother tried to set her up. And best of all, by going, she could learn more about probate without incurring an hourly rate.

They went to a steakhouse in midtown where Sol

sometimes took clients, usually important ones. The hatcheck girl took his coat and Andrea took several matchbooks. They were seated at once, a very nice table far from the toilets. Out of habit, the attorney ordered a porterhouse and Andrea ordered the filet. Sol was glad the meal was on the firm.

The two talked mostly about the estate which, apart from her nieces and nephews who were so cute but were such a handful, was all that seemed to interest the lovely Andrea. That was fine. At least she didn't say—not once—"Yes, Bush is a *putz*, but he's good for Israel."

As it happened, during the course of the meal, Sol noticed a pea fly from Andrea's fork while she gestured with her hands—something that, miraculously, had not previously caused large chunks of steak or mashed potatoes to become airborne.

The pea bounced in and out of the pea-pod wine and landed with an audible plop on the young woman's blouse, raising such a shriek one would have thought the Wailing Wall had been moved to 45th Street.

"This will leave a stain!" Andrea cried, drawing the attentions of the waiter with a damp napkin and the maitre d' who offered a moist towelette.

"That will smear it!" she exhorted nasally, knocking away the waiter. "And that will cause permanent discoloration!" she sneered at the other.

No one but a true Jewish American Princess could be so firm, so ungrateful, and at the same time so frightening, thought Sol with a mixture of admiration and familiarity.

And then the attorney, wise to the ways of the world, uttered the magic words that not only saved the night but won Andrea's heart.

"Let's go," he said, rising.

"Where?" she asked, still in a panic.

"To buy you a new blouse," said he. "At Saks."

At once a calm settled upon her, like the arrival—five days late—of her period. Sol asked for doggie bags and then they went up Fifth Avenue where they bought the blouse; after which he proposed and they continued to Tiffany's at Andrea's insistence, even though there were many fine jewelry shops much closer.

So at last the attorney took a wife, a true and real Jewish American Princess. As for the pea, Sol had removed it from the blouse once a new one had been purchased and folded it away in his handkerchief.

After the honeymoon, he placed it in a clear Lucite paperweight, which he kept on his desk at home. For it so annoyed Andrea, yet amused him, to tell others that after searching the world over, he had finally met his wife while taking a pea.

Little Red Pesadica Sheitel

ot so long ago—at least, if you're as old as *Bubbe* Sarah who is ninety and has wooden teeth—in a certain *shtetl* in a remote place where Jews were then still allowed, lived a little girl, the prettiest creature who ever had mud on her.

Her mother was excessively fond of this girl, and her grandmother—the aforementioned Sarah—doted on her even more. *Bubbe* was so devoted, in fact, that she made her granddaughter a little red *sheitel* to wear over her head when she was out in public to prepare her for the day when she, like mother and grandmother, would be a happily married, then widowed, woman.

So beautiful was the wig that people called the child Red, for that was easier to call out than Berura Chaviva Ashkenazy.

One day, not long before Pesach, Red's mother made some *matzoh* and said to her daughter, "Go and take these to your grandmother, who suffers from some *farshlepteh krenk* and is too ill to be with us for the holiday."

Red was relieved to discover that this was a lingering illness and not a houseguest with an unwieldy name like her own.

Little Red Pesadica Sheitel set out immediately for the village where her grandmother lived—on the outskirts, since they could get a better price there on a hut.

"Be careful!" her mother called after her. "*Bubbe's shtetl* has *pogroms!*"

Thinking that would make a wonderful song, Red made up lyrics as she romped through the woods.

> Bubbe's shtetl *has* pogroms—oy, oy, oy, oy, *oh!*
> *She tells the Russians,* "Gai tren zich!"—oy, oy, oy, oy, *oh!*
> *With a Cossack here, a* shoymer *there,*
> *Here a* zetz, *there a* shtup, *everywhere such* tsuris . . .

As Red neared the village, she met with a Cossack on horseback, who asked to see her papers because that was his job. As he looked at them, he had it in mind to grab Red's unleavened Hebraic loaves and

make a meal of them. But he dared not, for some *daveners* were nearby in a glade, alternately praying and yelling about whether to send a letter to the tsar, not because it would stop the *pogroms*, but to have something in writing about the destruction of property for insurance purposes. Though he did not fear the Jews when they were eating or abed, the Cossack did not like to cross them when they argued.

The Cossack returned Red's YWHA membership card and asked where she was going. The poor child, who did not know that it was dangerous to stay and talk to the ruffian, said, "I am going to see my grandmother with *matzohs* for her Seder."

"Did you say Seder or *zayde*?" the Cossack asked.

"'Seder,'" she replied. "My *zayde*, Nachem Levitchsky, is with God."

The Coassack knew the name. Being a watchman of the road, he also knew the two-timer was with his other family in Kiev. But that didn't matter. The point was, the old *karóva* Sarah was alone.

"Well," said he, "I'll let you be on your way."

"*Danken*," she replied.

The Cossack rode as fast as he could, taking the shortest path—stopping only for coffee since, curse her, the girl's words had put it in his mind. He did not get a donut or holes, however, so as not to spoil his appetite.

Meanwhile, Red went a roundabout way, entertaining herself by making up more songs, admiring her *sheitel* in every pond she passed, talking to the *daveners* until they began to ask what smelled so good—and taking a brief nap because this was quite a *shlep*.

It was not long before the Cossack arrived at the old woman's house. He knocked at the door: tap, tap.

"*Gai avek!*" she yelled over the radio. "I'm listening to my stories!"

"But it is I, your grandchild Little Red Pesadica Sheitel," cooed the Cossack, in a soft voice like the one he had used when he and Taras Bulba were on a very long ride across the steppes that took weeks.

"I'm in bed!" the woman said. "Use the key in the *mezuzah*."

The Cossack retrieved the iron key and opened the door. He immediately fell upon the good woman because she had left her slippers right in the middle of the rug. Knocked unconscious by the hilt of his saber, the woman was dragged from her bed and stuffed in a closet.

"I'll have *chaloshes* from the camphor smell!" she cried, waking.

The Cossack went back and stuffed a *shmatta* in her mouth. Then he put on her nightclothes, crawled into the bed, pulled the covers up to his beard, and waited.

Soon afterwards came a knock at the door: tap, tap.

"Who's there?" the Cossack asked, now imitating the frail *bubbe*.

"It is I, your *shayne pitseleh!*"

"Come in, Yourshana!" said the Cossack, for he was unschooled in the language of the Jews.

Upon hearing the unfamiliar pronunciation, Little Red Pesadica Sheitel was at first afraid. But knowing her grandmother to be occasionally *farblondget*, she entered and approached the bed. Red decided not to say, yet, the question she had promised to ask.

"I have some Pesach *matzohs* my mother sends you," Red said.

"Put them upon the table and get into bed with me."

Her grandmother said nothing about being careful not to leave crumbs, which seemed very strange. Nonetheless, Red got into bed. Though the beard was unchanged, perhaps a little fuller, the girl was amazed to see how big her grandmother's belly looked in her nightclothes.

"*Bubbe*, what big *kishkes* you have!"

"All the better for you to bounce on, my dear."

Bounce on? *Bubbe* was always telling her to behave or she'd have to write a hundred times, "I must not roughhouse." And she had said *my dear*! That was just too *waspy*.

"Bubbe, what big eyes you have!" Red said next.

"All the better to see with, my child."

My child? What was this, Tolstoy?

"*Bubbe*, what big teeth you have got!" Red went on.

"All the better to eat your breads with, my little kosher snack!"

Breads and not *matzohs*? Snack and not *nosh*?

This was not her *bubbe*, and Red called to the *daveners* who stood just outside, having come along to see if the old woman might join them for a local Seder, for she was without *mishpucha* and they were without *bubbes*. The *lantsleit* fell upon the Cossack and beat him with candlesticks and heavy skillets, two items of which there was no shortage. The attack left him broken and moaning and still dressed in the nightgown, which is how the authorities found him. The *chutzpenik* was booted from the Cossack corps and sent to Siberia, where at least he was warm in *bubbe*'s heavy clothes.

"The moral of the story," Red's mother told her when she returned, "is that men are not to be trusted—not even Jewish men, for who but the *daveners* could have eaten the *matzohs* you left on the table, as your *bubbe*'s teeth were still in a glass?"

Goldie's Lox and the Three Bagels

Little Goldie was a very pretty girl from Brooklyn who lived, once upon a time, in Denmark, which was a country very far away. She hadn't wanted to leave her neighborhood, but her father was a lawyer, now assigned to the World Court, and living here was better than living in France or in the Netherlands, where Jews had never fared too well.

"At least in Scandinavia, we are able to get good lox," Goldie's mother Sylvia announced with rare optimism, though not comprehending why the Danes called it *smoked salmon*. What Sylvia regretted, however, was that they couldn't get a good bagel anywhere in Copenhagen.

"We live on Sjaeland, not Sjewland," Hesh Gutbaum reminded his wife and daughter.

"We live in Denmark," Sylvia grumped, "and *a klog iz mir*, we can't even get a good Danish!"

"True, but how about that wienerbrød?" Hesh said, not helping matters at all.

One Sunday morning, just a few weeks after they arrived, Goldie was sitting on the hearth rug of their small one-bedroom place, writing to grandma for money as her mother complained how *this much rent* would have bought them a townhouse on 62nd Street and stubbornly calling it *an apartment* and not a *flat*, which she insisted was a broken tire and not a place where normal people lived.

And yet, being a Jewish woman however young, Goldie herself was not without complaint. Deciding that she couldn't take another bite of anything on rye bread, let alone lox, the plucky young girl decided to try to find a baker, somewhere in what her mother called this *goyisha nightmare*, one who could be instructed on how to make a bagel.

Announcing that she was going to mail her letter, Goldie trotted out the door, down two flights of steps, and onto the street, which wasn't called a street but a *plads*. Dropping the letter in the mailbox, Goldie kept walking. It was the first time the young girl had been out on her own, but she figured that as long as she paid attention to where she was going, she wouldn't get lost.

It didn't take but two minutes for Goldie to end up at a canal called Peblinge sø which was a lot like the East River if you took away the big bridges, the joggers, cafès the interesting skyline, and anything that might belong to the last two centuries. After standing there and thinking how fishy and rotten Denmark smelled, the girl decided to go home. Unfortunately, every corner in Copenhagen was called Hovedbanegarden or Ny Carlsberg Glyptotek or something similar, instead of normal names like Flatbush and Crown Heights. Goldie got them confused and suddenly realized that she had no idea which of these streets she had taken to get here.

"Stay calm and think," she said, imitating the *yeshiva bochers* she used to hear in the streets and not having to lower her voice to do so. "You live on some major *ongepatcheket plads*. If you go back toward town, you'll run into it."

Emboldened, not to mention sick of people smiling at her just because she was a little girl out on her own—in Prospect Park, only *mieskeits* with scruffy jowls did that—Goldie turned and headed in the general direction from whence she had come.

As luck would have it, on the way she passed a baker's shop. And catching her eye from a corner of that shop was a familiar shape.

"Could it be?" she wondered.

Goldie tried the handle but it didn't budge. Then she noticed a little clock sign in the window indicating that it would be open at ten o'clock. That was a half hour away and, being young and Jewish, Goldie didn't feel like waiting. Using bobby pins the way her Uncle Bugsy had showed her, Goldie picked the lock, stepped inside, and pulled the shade behind her.

At once, a familiar smell caused her nostrils to perk. Her big brown eyes settled upon the display case she had seen. In it were three glorious circular objects, each one larger than the one beside it.

"Bagels!" she cried and ran for the counter as she had seen her mother do during unadvertised sales at Macy's.

Goldie picked up the nearest bagel, the smallest one, and found it to be quite hard. She rapped on the counter, causing small chunks to fall off.

"This one is fit only for pigeons and the homeless," she said, returning it to the glass shelf.

She picked up the second bagel, which cracked

for it was brittle on the outside like Uncle Bugsy's slicked-back hair.

"If I had a microwave, maybe," she said and put it back.

Finally, she picked up the largest bagel that was a little hard when she squeezed but promised freshness within. Opening her mouth wide and biting, she was rewarded with a familiar doughy texture and the happy taste of home.

"This one is just right!" she said and then smiled as she proceeded to consume the entire thing, so utterly content that she had not even thought to look for a *shmear*.

Finishing the treat and tired from the long walk and the unexpected *fress*, Goldie next looked around for someplace to rest. There were three chairs in the small dining area, and she tried them.

The first, a high chair, was too small to fit even part of her *tush*. The second, a regular-sized wooden chair, was too hard. The third, a large comfy arm-chair like the one they had in Starbucks, was perfect. She snuggled into it, and within moments was asleep, dreaming of finding a twenty-dollar bill on the floor of the N Train and spending it before her mother made her put it in the bank.

"When I was your age, I put all my babysitting money in the Dime," she heard Sylvia drone in her dream. "Also we had passbooks, not websites with pin numbers. You could hold it in your hand!"

"I know, ma."

"And we collected for UNICEF," dream Sylvia went on. "Who knew those children would grow up to hate us?"

Though oddly disturbed, Goldie's slumber was so sound that she never heard the door open or the baker walk in with three guests: Mr. Halevy, Mrs. Halevy, and Master Halevy, the elder Halevy being an international investment banker from Tel Aviv.

"I have followed the recipe you provided," the baker was saying. "I'm sorry you could not come by yesterday, when they were fresh—"

"Your Sabbath is today," the accountant said. "Our Sabbath was yesterday."

In a nation of blondes, thought Mr. Halevy, everyone is a potential village idiot.

"Well," said the baker, "if these are satisfactory, I will make as many as you want for the Bear Stearns reception."

The baker and his guests stopped by the display case. As one, they gasped.

"‏יא אללה‎!" cried Master Halevy, who spoke no Danish, for when would he ever use it again?

"I don't know who broke your bagel!" the baker replied, inferring from the boy's tears and desperate grip on the hem of his mother's coat what was amiss.

But Master Halevy was not the only complainer.

"Who broke my bagel?" Mrs. Halevy demanded.

"*Sha!*" her husband snapped. "At least you two have bagels!"

"How could this have happened?" the baker lamented, though he secretly suspected some Jew had been tipped off and snuck in.

Undisturbed by the shouting of the three Jews, but unaccustomed to the soft voice of the baker, Goldie stirred from her slumber.

"I dreamt I went to Manderley . . ." Goldie muttered, stretching. She froze when she saw the baker. "Maxim?" she said, still not entirely awake, though one gentile *alter kocker* staring at an underage girl looks like another, not dissimilar from those men in Prospect Park.

Then, noticing the man's apron, Goldie remembered where she was.

She sat upright with a start and was now visible to the baker and his guests.

"I was right!" the baker blurted.

Rather than spin a *megillah*, Goldie jumped from the chair, ran past the startled group, and charged unmolested through the open door. For if there's one thing a Jewish woman of any age knows instinctively to do, it is to charge.

Meanwhile, smitten by the lovely young girl and noticing that she had lost a shoe on the way out, Master Halevy released his mother's garment and went to pick it up.

Mrs. Halevy slapped him hard on the back of his head.

"*Gotteniu*, drop it!" she cried. "You don't know where it's been!"

Never stopping to see if the three from Bear Stearns were in pursuit, Goldie ran and ran and ran until she could run no farther. And when at length she fell down in a heap, where should she find herself but right back at her flat. She went inside, but did not tell her mother about the bagels. If she did, then Sylvia would want to go there, and the baker would ask how she knew; then it would be *potches in tuchas* for the young girl.

Alas, Goldie's mother spanked her anyway for the missing shoe, which they would now have to buy marked up by these Danish *goniffs*. Still, it had been quite an adventure, one that Goldie would tell her children, her children's children, and her therapist for years to come.

The Cantor's New Shmattas

nce upon a time there lived a *chazzan* whose only worry in life was to look as elegant as he sounded.

It wasn't enough for Paul Ehrlich to wear just a four-panel black hat. His had to have six panels and a color pattern. One scarf *tallis* was not enough for him; he also had a full-length one, hand embroidered. His *tefillin* bags were covered with silver leaf, and his *yarmulkes* were blue suede or black leather or white silk, held with a solid gold bobby pin, which was foil embossed so that he shined brighter than the *ner tamid* itself.

And his robes? Crushed black velvet with red satin lining.

Inscriptions on the restroom walls referred to *Chazzan* Elvis and *Rugelach* Paul. But the cantor never saw these, for he had his own bathroom in his study in the back of the *shul*.

Chazzan Ehrlich changed his liturgical clothes several times a day and loved to show them off to the congregation, which had paid for his wardrobe. Why the trustees tolerated his extravagance was explained by the fact that their mothers and grandmothers had a thing for him, as if he were Liberace of the Jews. Why the rabbi stood for it was a mystery, though rumor had it that one of the cantor's *yarmulkes* contained a camera, which had captured him in an impious moment involving a menorah and several members of the B'nai B'rith.

However, *Chazzan* Ehrlich had to pay for his own suits. As it happened, the *karger* owned the first nickel he had ever earned singing in a bathhouse, for he was very, very, very cheap. So it came to pass that he wrote in the temple newsletter asking to buy name brands at wholesale or below—Armani would be nice, he added—not for his own vanity, he said, but so the High Holy Day services should have a certain *shaynen*.

Well, there were two tailors who did not much care for the cantor's high-handed *shtoltz* and decided to take advantage of it. Their scheme broke several of God's Commandments, but then *Adonai* had not yet had the pleasure of meeting Paul Ehrlich, and if He had, He would forgive them.

"We are two *vunderlich* tailors," said one tailor as they introduced themselves. "We have devoted many years of study—"

"Like Talmudists, for we are men of the cloth," interrupted the second.

"And have discovered a way to weave a cloth so light and fine that it looks invisible," continued the first. "In fact, it is invisible to anyone who is too stupid and incompetent to appreciate its quality."

The cantor seemed vaguely disinterested, as when people told him what a wonderful voice he had, for at such times he wanted to say, "Tell me something I don't know!"

"I know there are miraculous fabrics on the market," the cantor said. "But at what cost?"

"*Putz!*" said one, hitting his own head with a palm. "Did I not mention that this miraculous fabric costs less than a modest party platter?"

"*Tahkeh*, you did not!" the cantor replied.

Chazzan Ehrlich gave the two men money from the administrative office *pushkeh* in exchange for their promise to begin working on the suit immediately. Rosh Hashanah was near, and he wanted to look his most grand. Plus, he was eager to discover which of those congregants were ignorant and undeserving of an inscription in the book of life.

A few days later, after Sabbath services, the cantor asked an usher, Mr. Birnbaum, to stop by the tailor shop on his way home to see how the work was proceeding. It wasn't exactly on Mr. Birnbaum's route, but the cantor promised him a bonus *mitzvah* if he stopped.

"God keeps score, you know," the cantor said.

The *tsedrait* old man was happy for the insight, the blessing, and a dollar for the extra gas it would take.

Pulling up to the shop on Main Street, Mr. Birnbaum was warmly welcomed by the two scoundrels.

"We're almost finished," said one, holding his empty hands palms up. "See?"

The old man stared. He saw fingers that looked like they had never worn a thimble, so fair they were, and palms that were red for some unknown reason.

"Admire the colors, feel the softness!" said the other tailor.

The senior citizen squinted to see the fabric that was not there. He reached out and could feel nothing—except the perspiration that soiled his own underarms.

"I see *bupkis*," he thought. "But if I tell that to the cantor, he will think me stupid! He will take back the *mitzvah*, and worse, he may deem me too incompetent to show people to their seats on Rosh Hashanah, and I will not be able to save the ones nearest the exit for my sister Ethel who is big and waddles!"

And so Mr. Birnbaum said to them, "*Mazel tov!* Very nice."

The two men bowed graciously, but when he left, the *gantser goniffs* resumed the high fives that had left their palms so red and sore.

"What a maroon!" cried one tailor through his tears.

Before heading home, Mr. Birnbaum called the cantor's cell phone and left a message assuring him that the suit was like nothing he'd ever seen.

"In fact," Mr. Birnbaum added, "you won't believe your eyes!"

The message pleased the cantor no less than Abraham getting that timely and welcome message from God.

Just before the High Holy Days, the cantor finally received word that his new suit was ready. He bade the men bring it right over.

"I shall be more resplendent than Joseph and his coat of many colors," the cantor thought giddily as he awaited the arrival of the two tailors.

The tailors arrived with a large, shiny box containing the fruits of their labor, which showed more Fruit of the Loom than labor.

"Here it is, eminence," said one, extending his arms as if something were draped upon them. "We have worked night and day, but the most beautiful suit in the world is ready for the New Year. Look at the colors and feel how fine it is!"

The cantor's features puckered like his fat Aunt Jenny's elbow, for he did not see any colors, nor could he feel any cloth. That meant he was ignorant and uncultured. He felt dizzy and *farmisht*, like the time he ate *gefilte* fish from a store that was still called Daitch.

However, *Chazzan* Ehrlich suddenly realized that no one would know he could not see the fabric.

"Not so *partatshnek*," the cantor said, for he was incapable of actually giving anyone a compliment.

"Will you honor us by trying on the suit, in case it needs altering?"

The cantor obliged with a courtly nod. He stripped off his clothes and let the tailors help him on with the new suit. When they were done—for he assumed they were, since the men stood back to admire their handiwork—*Chazzan* Ehrlich studied himself in the full-length mirror he kept in his office and in the other set in the ceiling so that he should see himself as God did. The cantor felt embarrassed by what he saw, but it passed as the men dutifully checked the sleeves and cuffs.

"Perfect!" said one.

"You wear clothes like no one we have ever met!" gushed the other.

"Yes, this does look very good on me," the cantor said, trying to sound comfortable.

"Then you will wear it on the High Holy Days?" one of the tailors asked to confirm.

"Tishrei 1 will not pass without the unveiling," he assured them.

"He means Tushrei 1," one of them giggled behind his hand.

"And his unveiling!" chuckled the other.

On the eve of the New Year, the cantor removed his suit from the box in which they had so carefully repacked it. He slipped it on as he had watched the men do and then adorned himself with his *tallis* and six-panel black hat. However, concerned that the *tallis* covered too much of his magnificent suit, he removed it and went out with just the hat.

By now, word of the suit had spread thanks to

THE CANTOR'S NEW SHMATTAS

that *yenta* Mr. Birnbaum. The congregants knew that not being able to see it meant they were *zhlubs*, or worse. At last, a hush fell over the packed *shul* as *Chazzan* Ehrlich stepped onto the *bimah* and stood before the Ark, facing the congregation. The rabbi had also emerged, though he was not looking at the worshipers.

Everyone sat in silence until the wide-eyed rabbi said, "*Shalom aleichem*—and just look at the cantor's new clothes!"

"Fair as a *maidel's punim*!" yelled one.

"Look at the colors!" shouted another.

"I have never seen anything like it!" offered one more.

As they all struggled to conceal their disappointment at not being able to see the suit, a little boy cried out: "Hey! I see the cantor's shaved *baitsim*!"

There was a moment of silence as heavy as a fruitcake, and soon others began to yell, "The boy is right! The cantor is *meshugeh*!"

"And naked!"

Of course, the cantor realized that the people were right, but he couldn't admit that. He excused himself, saying that he'd forgotten his *tallis*, and returned with the full-length one. And he also brought the *shofar*, which he held before him throughout the entire service and afterward at the receiving line where no one shook even his free hand.

As he stood revealed before everyone, a vain fool, only Mr. Birnbaum laughed and said, "God does indeed keep score!"

Jake and Mr. Bienstock

nce upon a time there was a widow who lived in a very modest split-level with her son Jake. Jake's father Bennie had left them not well-off, thanks to term insurance he bought from a TV commercial, and their only possession of any worth was the vintage T-Bird, for Bennie liked to *patchkies* around with old cars.

Alas, with gas prices what they were, Jake's mother had no choice but to sell the car and buy a Kia. She sent Jake to an antique car show at the mall to try to get a good price. Now, Jake knew from the *Talmud* but not from people. No sooner did he pull up than a man eating a *bialy* and making a face, for the *nosh* was plain, approached and offered him stock tips in exchange for the car.

"I'm to give you a car for financial advice?" Jake asked.

"What will a one-time sale get you, *bubbee*? A few dollars?" the big man asked. "These tips will provide dividends to keep you and your mother comfortable until Shavuous in the year 6000."

Jake agreed, and the big man told him where to invest what little was left of their money. When he returned home, he told his mother, who cried out "*Iz brent mir ahfen hartz!*" as the tips were for shell corporations owned by a shyster landlord named Mr. Bienstock. "Your father, may he rest in peace, also bought tips from that *shvindeler*!"

Humiliated, and his bowels constricted in terror by his mama's wrath, Jake vowed to recover their car. Learning that the tycoon lived in a mansion high on a mountain, Jake packed some leftover cold cuts and began the slow ascent along a steep dirt path, the only approach that wouldn't bring him to the big front gate, which was so large it had gold-leaf pictures of a *shtetl* on the outside—life size.

What a journey, one that could have taken him to the Borsht Belt and back three times over! Finally, Jake came to the backdoor where deliveries were made. Picking up a crate marked Howard, Fine & Howard, he walked boldly into the mansion where he immediately set his burden down, already being *farmutshet* from the climb and being unaccustomed to lifting.

No sooner had he set the bottles down than he was approached by a *zoftig* woman with too much makeup, whom he recognized at once as Fifi Farfolen, a onetime star of the Yiddish theater.

"Where is the regular seltzer man, Larry?" she asked, then gasped. "I hope it isn't his newborn Jo!"

"Jo is fine," Jake said. "In fact, Larry had to interview *moyels* today."

Fifi's big eyes narrowed. "The *kelyner* is a daughter!"

"*Oy*," Jake blurted, cursing the genetic makeup that made him always say a little more than was necessary.

Once more the rage of a Jewish woman had affected the young man's *kishkes*, only this time they opened wide like the Red Sea.

"Who are you and why are you here?" the woman asked, picking up a cleaver as she sniffed the air. "And how dare you bring fatty cold cuts that Mr. Bienstock isn't allowed to have on account of his high cholesterol?"

"Sha! It's very lean, I assure you," Jake said quickly.

The woman shook the cleaver menacingly.

"I . . . I am but a young man to whom Mr. Bienstock gave a *shpiel* in order to steal his car," he answered. "I only came to get it back."

"*Iz brent mir ahfen hartz!*" Fifi groaned.

It seemed not at all strange that this *yachneh* had uttered the same phrase as his mother, though he was surprised to see such a woman in such wealthy surroundings wearing the same housecoat.

Fifi lowered the cleaver. "My husband is so cheap I am forced to order from J. C. Penney, yet for himself he buys another car!"

"Your husband?"

She nodded sadly.

"I don't know why you stand for that," Jake said, an idea occurring to him, even though he was conflicted by feelings of *carpe diem* and wanting to *platz*.

"We have a prenup," Fifi explained. "My matchmaker was not very good. My lawyer was worse."

"*Ech hob dir in pishachs!*" Jake said.

Fifi frowned. "He should go to urine?"

"To hell," Jake replied.

"That would be *in drerd*," Fifi corrected.

"Ah!" Jake smiled, for she had taken the bait. "You see, Fifi? You should be a *chazenteh*, for you have much to offer."

"You make me *farklempt*," the woman said with a

little smile, which on those vast red lips looked like
kosher franks ready to pop. "I cannot leave, for a
cantor would not have me. But—come."

"Where?" Jake asked innocently.

"Perhaps I can help you recover your car."

Kvelling over his own clever ruse, Jake followed the
woman as she took a key from her apron, opened a
heavy door, and took him down a flight of stairs to
a huge underground garage where there were over
fifty vehicles ranging from a Model T to My Mother
the Car. Jake thought Ms. Sothern looked very
good, though she needed dusting. The only German
or Austrian car was a vintage Volkswagen that had
been converted to a toilet.

"My husband goes in it, but does not flush," Fifi
apologized, waving her hand in front of her face. "It
is a warning that our people should stay away from
them."

A hurried look through the room did not reveal
the T-Bird. But at the far end of the room was a
magnificent solid-gold Corvette.

"There's my car!" he said, running toward it.

"Which one?" Fifi asked, a little *tsemisht*.

Jake did not answer. He ran to the pegboard

where the keys were hanging like at Grossingers, pressed the garage door opener, and scurried quick like a bunny into the sports car.

"*Boichik*, you must be mistaken," Fifi yelled. "Bienstock has had that car since before you were born—"

"I can't hear you!" Jake called back, pointing at the front of the garage. "The door is noisier than my *zayde*'s snoring!"

Jake could hear even less when he started the engine of the Corvette, which purred like in the movies. Yet even that was not enough to drown the roar that came from the stairwell.

"Fifi Farfolen—I smell Pastrami from a *yiddisher chaver*!"

Jake froze. His frightened eyes—again, like a bunny—met those of Fifi.

"It's just the seltzer man who stopped first by the deli!" Fifi shouted as she ran to the stairs to stop her husband.

But the highly seasoned smell of smoked beef was too powerful. Mr. Bienstock crashed through his wife like Moshe Dayan through the Golan Heights in '67. Seeing him coming, Jake floored the gas pedal, threw the car into drive, and flew through the door.

"*Ech hob dir in drerd!*" Mr. Bienstock screamed, which Jake half expected.

Easily steering the Corvette along the dirt path, Jake could tell that the owner had gotten rid of the single-disc front calipers and had upgraded to the dual-piston units. It amazed him that he knew that, since he had never even looked under the hood of a car, preferring his *Talmudic* studies, which also explained why at thirty-two he was alone and living at home.

As the sports car thumped, bumped, and weaved down the path, Jake glanced in the rearview mirror. He was just in time to see Mr. Bienstock—as unaccustomed to the outdoors as he was—catch his big, clumsy foot in the exposed root of a Judas tree, of all things. Mr. Bienstock fell like the walls of Jericho, only in one big piece, his thick flesh being bruised and torn over and over as he dropped.

"*A shvartz yor*! Collect those *rents*," Jake shouted out the window, giving himself *nachas* once again and flashing his brights at the *nishtgutnick* as he rolled by.

Jake reached the bottom of the mountain and drove home. His mother was delighted to see him, not only because her Jakey was home in time for dinner, but because he had recovered the very Corvette his father had *futzed* with for years before foolishly giving it to Mr. Bienstock for a tip about oil wells outside Tel Aviv.

While his mother found slices of tongue that weren't so green, Jake rushed to the car show where he sold the Corvette for a small fortune. He and his mother never again ate food that was *shtark gehert*, and Mr. Bienstock was never seen again, for he had landed on the main road where he was struck by a BMW.

He may have been a *shtunk*, but Mr. Bienstock was right about those cars.

Rapunseltov

here were once a man and a woman who dwelt in the Holy Land and had long wished for a child—in vain.

"Wishing is nice, but *shtupping* is what makes it happen," the husband told their accountant, who had just suggested that a little deduction might help the innkeeper get out of debt. "My wife seems more interested in gazing out the kitchen window than in tending to the *matzoh* balls, if you take my meaning."

The wife's preoccupation was because from this window could be seen a splendid garden beside a great pool. Both were attached to the palace of a wealthy emir, who himself was not chopped liver—tall and swarthy like Omar Sharif in *Funny Girl*, not *shlumpy* like her husband.

One day, right before Pesach, the woman was standing by the window and looking into the garden when she saw a tree rich with the most beautiful apples. So she said to her husband, "If you don't get me a fresh apple for the *charoset*, I shall die!"

"*Bubeleh*," said her husband, "if I go into that man's garden to steal and I am caught, then I shall die—"

His wife interrupted as usual to say, "Get it for me and we will couple this very night."

"Which apple?"

"That one," she said, pointing to a fat one on top.

Unfortunately, no sooner had the overeager husband set foot in the emir's garden and pulled the full, green apple from the branch, then the *k'nacker* himself emerged from his palace. The great man unsheathed a scimitar and strode toward the husband, who hadn't seen such a tool since his nephew's *bris* and, wouldn't you know it, pointed at the same place.

"You trespass," the emir remarked contemptuously.

"My gracious neighbor comes to the point," the husband said admiringly. "My own people lack that paucity of expression—"

The emir noticed a bulge in the husband's pants and pushed the sword closer. It struck apple.

"And you steal," the emir said. "Why?"

"A *broch*," lamented the husband. "I came of necessity, which as a man with many wives, you may not understand. My own precious lamb, who even now stands in the window reading our will, felt the need to include your apple in our Seder. This desire was so great that she agreed to lie with me if I but obtained one."

The emir lowered his blade and allowed his anger to soften. And he said to the husband, "I will allow you to keep the apple—and your life—on one condition."

"Speak it!" the husband exclaimed, aware that he was in no position to *hondle*.

"You must give me the child that issues from the union with your wife," he said. "It shall be well treated, I promise."

"Can I also have some horseradish for my wife to use in the moro?" the husband asked, finding his strength.

"One small root for your wife," he agreed.

"Thank you," said the husband, ignoring the little *kibbitz*. "Yet great sir, I have seen many children frolicking in the pool. Why do you wish this one?"

"So that I will one day inherit your inn and turn it into a cabana."

That made sense.

The husband agreed to the deal, thinking he had outsmarted the emir, for tonight he would not plant his seed in his wife but would hold off and deposit it after his hero Onan had done.

Nine months later they had a daughter.

The wife named her Rapunzeltov, assuming the emir would not accept a child with such an odd name. However, that did not deter Ali bin Nuzzer' q'fehtisef.

True to his word, the husband turned the newborn over to the emir, assuring his wife that their neighbor was just going to babysit for a while.

"What is *a while*?" the wife asked.

"About eighteen years, and why not?" the husband asked. "*Tahkeh,* if she has your teeth, who can afford braces?"

Not wishing any man to have Rapunzeltov as his wife—and with her, the inn—the emir had her placed in a tower when she was thirteen, in a room that had neither stairs nor door, just a little window at the top. When the emir wanted to visit, he would call to his little *bubbee*, "Rapunzeltov, Rapunzeltov, let down your hair!"

You see, Rapunzeltov had beautiful long hair, fine

as gold spun by Rumpleforeskin. Whenever she heard the voice of the emir, she unfastened her tresses and let them fall to the ground so the emir could climb.

Now it came to pass that a doctor named Gershon, who still made house calls, passed by the tower. He saw Rapunzeltov in the window and, forgetting Mrs. Bloomburg's colonitis for the moment, stood and watched as Rapunzeltov let down her hair for the emir. After a few minutes the chieftain left, at which point Gershon went to the tower and cried: "Rapunzeltov, Rapunzeltov, let down your hair."

Almost immediately, down went the hair and up went the doctor.

At first Rapunzeltov was terribly frightened when a man whom her eyes had never yet beheld came through the window. But the doctor had a very nice bedside manner and warm hands, and Rapunzeltov lost her fear, among other things. When, hours later, he asked if Rapunzeltov would take him for her husband, she gave up the idea of one day marrying her hairdresser who, though a *faigelah*, gave a wonderful wash and set.

Alas, the emir saw what transpired because the window of his own tower was not ten feet away. Enraged, he went over after Gershon had left and—

snip, snap—cut off Rapunzeltov's golden hair. Then he took her from the palace, carried her into the desert, and left her at a tiny oasis far from any trade routes.

"Wait!" cried Rapunzeltov as he rode off on his camel. "I've been out of the sun—I'll burn!"

Upon reaching the palace, the emir sent a message to the Bloomburgs, where Gershon was still deep in his examination.

"Rapunzeltov is lost to you," wrote the emir. "I have cut her hair, and you will never see her again."

The doctor was immediately in such pain that even the considerable fee he collected from Mrs. Bloomburg could not chase it away. In his despair, he wandered from her home and kept on going, just like Edward G. Robinson in *The Ten Commandments*—who, ironically, was the only real Jew with a major role.

Gershon roamed in misery for many months (or at least nine), subsisting on cactus and the lollipops he carried for crying children, whom he'd rather have smacked. At length, the doctor happened to come to the oasis where Rapunzeltov had been left. He didn't recognize her at first, the sun having turned her the color of Benazir Bhutto, who Gershon always thought was much hotter than Princess Di, who he just didn't get.

There, Rapunzeltov lived with the twins to whom she had given birth.

Joyous, Rapunzeltov and Gershon were wed, and the family returned to the inn where they lived for a long time afterward, happy and contented and never selling to the emir even at a very good price.